I'll Protect You from the Jungle Beasts

MARTHA ALEXANDER

NEW YORK  THE DIAL PRESS

Copyright © 1973 by Martha Alexander
All rights reserved.
Library of Congress Catalog Card Number: 73-6015
Printed in the United States of America.
First Pied Piper Printing 1980

A Pied Piper Book
is a registered trademark of The Dial Press.
I'LL PROTECT YOU FROM THE JUNGLE BEASTS is published
in a hardcover edition by
The Dial Press, 1 Dag Hammarskjold Plaza,
New York, New York 10017
ISBN 0-8037-3900-1

FOR SCOTT M. S.

Oh, yes, Teddy, there are lions and tigers
and elephants in this forest – big ones. But don't
worry, I'll protect you from the jungle beasts.

Yes, they *are* fierce, but I won't let them
hurt you. Do snakes eat teddy bears? Well,
not if they have someone to protect them.

You really mustn't worry. That was a
very old lion. I could tell by his roar.

I'm sure he's toothless and too tired to
even run. And I can run like the wind.

Or I could hit him between
the eyes with my slingshot.

Don't be frightened, Teddy!

HA !HA! HA!

HEEE E E EE

HAHAHA

HA HA HAHA HA HA HAHAHAHA

I think that was a hyena. They *do*
have spooky laughs. No, I really don't
think they eat teddy bears.

Boys? Oh, I'm not sure. There's a big club.
I can smash him to bits if he comes near us.

No, I'm not frightened.

Well, I *thought* this was the path home.
Do you see any lights anywhere?

Lost?

Well, I don't know. I wish I'd brought
my compass with me.

You have what—a built-in home finder?
That must be something only teddy bears
have. A special kind of stuffing? Oh.

GRRR R
R RR R R
RRRRRRRR—
GRRRRRRR—

Yes, that was very close.
It must be enormous.

Shaking? Me? I must be
getting a fever or something.

If I get sick it might be hard to clobber
a big fierce animal. I always feel weak
when I have a fever.

Perspiration? That must be
from the fever I'm getting.

Boy, I wish I were filled with stuffing.
Then I wouldn't have this fever.

My knees are a little weak.
Lean on you? Oh, good.

You *are* strong. Your stuffing?
I wish *I* had special stuffing.

Oh, Teddy, I feel better already.
My fever seems to be going away, too.

Look! There's our house!

It's nice to be in our own bed again . . .

isn't it?

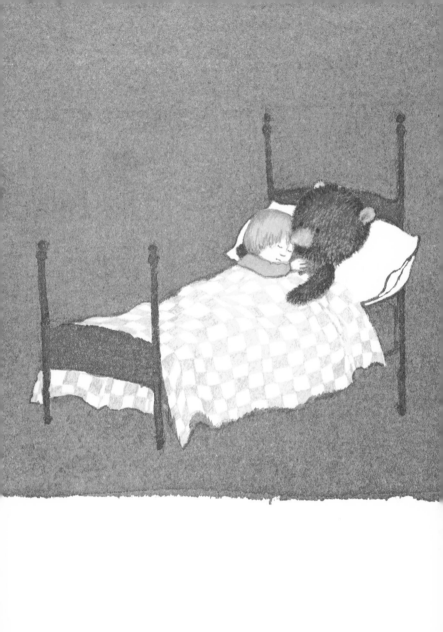

Good morning, Teddy!
How's your stuffing?